TOMORROW AND BEYOND

TOMORROW AND BEYOND

GWEN TOLIOS

Libra Chai

CONTENTS

Copyright Page

Cover Art by Gwen Tolios, assisted by Starry AI

Printed by Libra Chai

Self-Defense

"Are you sure you want to sit through the meeting? It might be... boring."

Britney looked past Mrs. Dolmski, who stood at the door to welcome attendees, to the room beyond. Britney's dad sat in the third row, drinking from a Coke bottle and leaning sideways.

Her neighbor might honestly think a city council meeting would bore a sixteen-year-old girl, but they both knew the real reason Britney may not want to be there – the knowledge it wasn't just Coke in the bottle Britney's dad drank from.

"I'll be fine," she pulled down her sleeves, tugged at her fingerless gloves. "I'll sit in the back."

"Okay, dear. Are you coming over after? I have a crockpot going." Mrs. Dolmski handed her an agenda.

Britney snuck another look at her dad. He didn't appear *too* drunk. "Maybe."

She took a seat in the far-left corner, pushing it closer to the off-white wall to put space between her and the next chair. She didn't bother reading the agenda. Britney knew the important topic. The one her dad ranted about. The one spawning rumors at school. The one she needed answers to.

Townsfolk continued to fill the room. Britney figured by the glances the council members slid each other this month's meeting was better attended than usual. Britney didn't gain a neighbor, but she felt boxed in all the same as the seats to the right and front of her filled.

She zipped up her coat. Slipped her phone into a pocket. If she had to leave, sneaking away using the gap she created would require a lot of concentration – best to reduce the worry about trailing sleeves or making sure she didn't drop something.

A mic tap drew eyes to the front of the room and conversations died down. Britney slumped low in her chair and rubbed a thumb over her knuckles, the fabric of her gloves smooth against her thumbprint but rough against the scabs underneath.

The council members introduced themselves, the TV camera in the aisle panning left to right across the front table. None of their names stuck in Britney's mind. She was too busy noticing the familiar people in the room: her father taking a drink of what was probably a rum and Coke, the greasy-haired woman beside him with a Starbucks cup most likely spiked with Irish cream, and Mrs. Dolmski in the back next to her husband.

Britney's gaze caught on a black-haired man in the front row whose thick jowls sparked something in Britney's memory. She tried to concentrate on his profile and remember, but blinked two minutes later to find herself staring at the clock and unable to recall when she turned her head.

"Since there's nothing to add to the agenda, let's move on to our first order of business-"

"No, let's skip ahead." The familiar-looking man stood up. Britney got an image of his face at the top of a set of grungy stairs. She shook it away.

A movie, she told herself. *A play. A TV show.*

"What is the city doing about this bar vandal?"

"Yeah!" Britney's dad added. He lurched to his feet, lips attached to the bottle. "Bad for business if I show up and there's nothing to drink."

A few people coughed awkwardly, and the city council members frowned at him for the interruption. No one called out the bottle. The entire town knew Stephen Gunther, knew his drinking habits. Britney wished for a hood to hide under.

"Mr. Gunther, Mr. Milan," a woman on the council said, "Both of you, please sit. We'll get to that later tonight."

"No," the man, Mr. Milan, said again.

Britney remembered the credit card bills on the kitchen table – Milan's Bar and Grill. Remembered the caller ID announcing her father's upcoming arrival, half-passed out in a taxi, and how she had to put him to bed. At ten, she was lucky to get him onto the couch. Now at sixteen, she had the strength to drag him up the stairs to his room.

Remembered fisting black napkins with "Milan's Bar & Grill" in white text in the corner and tossing them on the floor. Fists and fists and fists.

She opened and closed her hands, scabs catching on the fabric, and shook her head. *Dreams, a movie, a show.*

"My bar," Mr. Milan continued, "got vandalized *again* last night. That's the third time in six months. The city needs to stop this."

A murmuring of assent sounded from the audience; bar and restaurant owners grumbling over lost inventory and diners reminiscing about being told there was no wine to go with their dinner.

Britney had read all the police reports. Someone, or someones, breaking in and destroying all the alcohol bottles. Wine, beer, rum, tequila. Restaurants had been left intact. Bar owners, however, found glasses smashed, vinyl cushions bleeding stuffing, and cash registers in pieces.

Six months of businesses taking losses, installing locks, and sometimes closing. Six months of Britney shutting her eyes and imagining the sound of glass under her shoes, punching through windows, flipping a knife over and between her fingers.

She'd never do it. Didn't have the courage, couldn't make a fist. Didn't mean she hadn't laid in her bed and wondered. If her dad didn't drink, if the bars couldn't serve him, would she have purple handprints on her wrists? Would she tiptoe through the house? Eat dry Cheerios for lunch? Would she have ended up in the hospital eight months ago, hearing her dad explain to the doctors she'd been beaten up at school but having no memory of it, no memory of anything, and knowing it would be much more likely for *him* to give her the concussion and broken rib?

In her head, the glass under her shoes was uneven, her feet unbalanced as she ran out. Her fingernails ripped as she pried at the seams of cash register drawers.

"This is a sign we should be a dry town," someone called out.

Yes, Britney thought, running a fingertip over smoothly filed nails, *yes yes* even as she watched the people around her shake their heads.

"It should not!!" shrieked the woman sitting next to Britney's dad. Not a bar drinker, but one who bought bottles every week at the grocery store that Britney packed with shaking hands.

Conversation boiled up in the room, pockets of words popping and filling Britney's ears for a few seconds before the next one caught her attention.

A mic screech stopped the noise. "I encourage you to start a petition and go through the formal process of making Hayward a dry town if you wish, but that's not the point of today's meeting," the treasurer said. "As for this bar vandal, as Mr. Milan called him, it is a matter for the police to find the culprit. But we're prepared to discuss the installation of more lights on business streets, the establishment of a neighborhood watch, and hiring more officers."

"Do you think that will work?" Mr. Milan said, still standing with his arms crossed.

Britney watched her father say "It better," knowing the shape of those words even across the room. He said it a lot, about her promise to have dinner ready at a certain time, to improve her grades, to do the laundry.

"Yes, of course," someone else on the council answered. "This is unprecedented in our town and we all want it to stop, not just you, Mr. Milan. It's a priority for the city. Whoever is responsible for this will be caught and punished. We urge anyone with any information about these incidents to tell the police. Detective Dolmski is handling the case."

Terry Dolmski stood up from his seat next to his wife and waved to the crowd. The Dolmskis, the neighbors across the street who fed her dinner when cash was low and the fridge empty. Who let her hide in their living room. Who together kept her, and the town, safe.

Again, Britney imagined Mr. Milan's face at the top of the stairs, rudely woken from sleep and twelve feet above her. Heard him whisper, "You're a woman." Felt her hands against a door's crash bar, and two seconds later the bite of night air.

She sat on her hands, pressing her palms into the hard plastic. Tried to remember how exactly she bloodied them often enough to have scars.

What would her dad do, what would Mr. Dolmski do, if she walked up to them and whispered, *I think it's me.*

She blinked, suddenly outside the room and halfway down the block. Britney pulled off her gloves with her teeth. The scabs on her right knuckles were cracked, bright red beads of blood like grenadine on an oak bar top.

She heard footsteps. Britney turned to see Mrs. Dolmski walking toward her.

"Are you okay, Britney?"

Britney wanted to tell her, *Mr. Milan will tell Mr. Dolmski it's a woman. I think it's me. It must be me.*

She blinked and Mrs. Dolmski stood not feet away, but only an arm's length, concern in her eyes. "Britney?"

"You were right," she said, "It was a boring meeting."

End of the Century

When I wake up, my circuits feel malleable and after a few blinks to reset my HUD I see multiple body warning signs. If this heat keeps up, within two days my wiring will fry, my body will stop functioning, and without the generator in my chest to keep my cybernetic brain on, my neurons will stop firing and bring my death.

48 hours to live.

I do what any city girl would do. I blow off work, call my girlfriends, and we make our way to the End of the Century club.

We figure it's ironic. And hey, knowing I had only two days left I don't mind dipping in my savings for the cover fee. Or getting buzzed. I'm obviously not taking that trip to the Mariana Trench.

I meet Cindi, Xenon, and Nickle at the door to the club. There's a line to get in, but it moves fast through the chrome double doors and no one plugs their finger into the cash register.

"No cover, can you believe it?" Nickle asks.

Well, not like our money would matter in two days.

I wonder how all these people are going to fit in the club. It's a small, intimate place for celebrities based on the JPEGs I've seen. The answer becomes pretty clear once we walk in.

The club sits in the middle of a block and the walls into

the adjacent shops have been torn down to triple the dance floor. Anyone's guess who did the wrecking, the club owner or the dancers to relieve the tight press of bodies. Regardless, the club goers have taken over the extra space. Mods from the clothing store hang off the metal bodies of dancers and I bet all the good drugs from the neurosurgeon's have been discovered.

Xenon dives into the moving metallic bodies while the rest of us hang back and returns with a syringe of something. We share it between us before making our way to the thickest of the dancing, newly energized.

You can't do individual dance moves in the crowd, but the group sways and sporadic people thrust fists into the air or jump. The music is loud and thrumming, bass vibrations make our feet tingle while soft notes of electric strings play in my head over the club's Wi-Fi. I don't know if their staccato nature is the music or a side effect of my soft circuits. I don't care. I link arms with my girlfriends.

There's a camera in a corner of the ceiling, panning over the expanded club. No doubt, those on Mars are watching us. I imagine there will be tears and horror at the mass death and the heat from the expanding Sun cooks us all, but I feel a strong desire to show the people of Mars, and whoever else might watch in the future, that humans are a species full of life. Sure, we may have traded flesh bodies for mechanical ones centuries ago, but we have the same heart and soul. We are a species full of life and fun.

I concentrate on dancing and my friends. This newscast will go down in history and if we dance our best, are caught on camera for a millisecond, we'll be remembered in some way. This might be the end of my body and consciousness, but it doesn't have to be the end of me.

Confessions

"I highly, highly recommend it. It's got dragons."

"And time travel," I added.

"Yes! Time travel!" Kaylee's enthusiasm came through the phone and I smiled.

She drunk-rambled a lot, my sister, and like half of our conversations this one dipped into current reads and book recommendations. No doubt, in her cocktail-addled mind, Kaylee forgot she had mentioned this book to me last week. I'd tease her about it during our next call, but for now I let her words wash over me.

I didn't keep the conversation going aside from small noises. It was three-thirty in the morning and Kaylee's ringtone had woken me, but I heard my sister's voice so infrequently I never ignored a call.

My phone's speakers changed Kaylee's voice, made it higher, a little tinny. But if I closed my eyes and laid in bed, one ear pressed to my pillow and the other to my phone, it felt like I was seven and Kaylee had snuck into bed with me. We'd weave fantasy worlds based on our favorite shows, cuddle together to keep the winter's chill away.

When I was younger, Kaylee was my best friend. As we got older, that changed but she still was my go-to contact for a lot. I shared my date stories with her, work frustrations, my struggles at self-improvement and self-worth.

Kaylee shared... books. Sightseeing adventures. Sometimes ranted about climate change.

Terribly one-sided, I knew. But that's how sisters work, right? The big sis listens to and supports the younger one through her troubles. And the little sis keeps the older one young and annoys the heck out of her.

"You even listening?" Kaylee chastised.

I blinked my eyes open into the dark of my room. "I'm listening," I mumbled. "Sleepy."

"Sleepy, oh! I forgot you're four hours ahead of me. Sorry, sorry, I can hang up."

"No! Don't!" I pushed myself up to lean against the headboard and reached over to turn on my bedside lamp. The light blinded me, so I quickly turned it off. Instead, I fumbled for the remote to my battery-operated candles.

You fall asleep reading by candlelight and wake up to the fire alarm one time and you give up actual flames in the bedroom.

"Don't you have plans tomorrow?"

"Yeah," I admitted. "But I like listening to you. Even if it's just drunken book recs. Or complaints about your data."

"My data is always messy."

"You study climate change."

"It's so fascinating!" Kaylee went on about her current efforts in Alaska, and I smiled. I never understood most of the science she talked about, but it felt nice.

I found myself drifting off, but caught a burst of energy when Kaylee said my name.

"Kath?"

"Sorry, here."

"You should sleep."

"No!"

Kaylee's huff felt close enough to disturb my hair. "Just because *I'm* drunk doesn't mean you have to put up with me."

"I'm not putting up with you," I said, sinking back down into a reclining position. "Hearing your voice reminds me of family."

"We're sisters," Kaylee deadpanned.

Even with my eyes closed, I rolled them. "I mean, of *being* a family."

"We're always family," Kaylee said, confused.

"But we haven't been for a while," I muttered. "You don't come to visit."

Silence came through the line, and the lack of response made me wonder if I'd not spoken loud enough or if my sleepy words got lost between cell towers.

"Maybe Christmas," Kaylee eventually said.

"Maybe," I half-heartedly echoed.

After all, the past three Decembers, Kaylee hadn't come home.

Kaylee was always in great, amazing places to study receding glaciers and rising ocean temperatures, but they kept her away. Last year, her one-year program in Antarctica didn't allow holiday travel. The years before that, her grad school projects in Norway got in the way. At least Kaylee visited that summer for a bit.

I originally thought, since Kaylee was stateside for the first time in years, I would see her more frequently. But Easter was last month and she hadn't visited. And the plans for a 4th of July family reunion leaked out of Kaylee's memory too.

This Christmas, I felt ninety-percent sure, would again be Kaylee- less.

"I miss you," I sleepily confessed.

The *I miss you, too* I hoped for didn't come back to me through the speaker. In my sleepy state, the disappointment didn't hurt too much. That, or it was an old hurt I had gotten used to over the years.

After all, she never had the chance to say it in Antarctica because the bad network couldn't support non-essential calls. And while Kaylee worked on her master's degree abroad, the few times high international fees, time differences, and remote fieldwork allowed a call, she hadn't said she'd miss me. In fact, until Kaylee moved to Alaska earlier this year, I was lucky to hear her voice three times a year. The care packages I had sent were always reciprocated with e-mails weeks after USPS declared them delivered.

They never mentioned missing me either.

"I don't..." Kaylee trailed off and my heart clenched. "I don't miss you. At least, I don't think I do. Not like you."

"I'm too sleepy to understand that."

Kaylee's laugh filled my ear. "I might be too drunk to explain right. Remember your summer abroad?"

"Prince Edward Island. Tour guide," I mumbled.

"You called me or mom every day."

I remembered that. Of course, I did. My first time away from Tallahassee, I knew no one and wanted someone to talk to. And even after I bonded with co-workers, I was used to seeing and talking to family every single day. The sudden loss of that had been startling. Naturally, I picked up the phone every night.

"You never call me." I tried to keep the accusation out of my voice.

"I... I don't miss things," Kaylee admitted.

I pushed sleep away. Held on to the words. Kaylee never got personal.

"I have no urge to go home for Christmas," Kaylee continued. "Or Thanksgiving. To call you every week. I don't...I don't feel that bond with people. Not like you do."

She sighed, deep and heavy. "Maybe my mind's broken. I can't connect to people."

"What about the people you work with?" I asked.

"Well, I make friends fast. But it doesn't last. I don't talk to anyone from Norway, not unless they reach out. And from Antarctica, maybe one person. Out of sight, out of mind. Just, for people."

I tried to hide my wince by speaking through a fake yawn. "Isn't that lonely?"

"No." I imagined Kaylee shaking her head. "I never lack company. And never seek out particular people. Might be why I don't have a boyfriend," she confessed. "Maybe I'm incapable of missing people, of love. A low-class sociopath."

"Don't say that." I clutched my phone to my face. "It's not true."

Yet, the idea stayed with me. *Maybe I'm incapable of love.* I was scared Kaylee included me in that. She didn't love me, or our parents. Couldn't.

"I don't call you," Kaylee pressed. "I rarely write, be it text or e-mail. Just a lot of social media updates."

"I like every status."

"I always smile when I see that," Kaylee admitted.

"You always listen to me," I said. "When I have problems, you give me advice. When I want to rant, you let me go at it. Even if, even if you never do the same with me."

Silence drifted between us. I never admitted to Kaylee I had noticed that. I hoped the pain in my voice had been obscured by my returning grogginess. 4:01 AM, my watch read.

"Sorry," Kaylee whispered.

"It's okay," I whispered back. I felt more tired than before, due to both the hour and now the weight of our conversation. I pressed the button to turn off the candles. Sunk back down to my pillows.

"It's not okay for you. I can tell," Kaylee said.

"Hmmm. I'm just happy you call at all, even if it's drunk calls."

"I think I only call you when I'm drunk and it's late like this and I ramble about nothing. Every other time we talk, you're the one ringing me."

"Sounds right," I said around a yawn.

"I'll, I'll let you sleep. Night, Kath."

"Love you," I mumbled back, barely registering the beep of Kaylee hanging up.

No *love you too* shepherded me into sleep. It never came from Kaylee's lips, though I ended all our calls with the same phrase.

She called me when she was drunk; when she could have made a booty call or rambled to a local friend or collapsed into bed. Something in Kaylee's alcohol-filled brain did consistently say "Call Kath."

Before the thought could escape me, I typed out a quick message to Kaylee.

Am I the only one you drunk call?

I fell asleep before I got an answer, but I woke with my phone in my hand and a return text from Kaylee.

Yes

A Better Me

>>Destination?

Jiminy Cricket's

>>Accessing Webstore...

Welcome to Jiminy Cricket's! Looking for a conscience program?

Yes.

Wonderful! You came to the right place. Is there a type of program you are looking for?

Someone always active, consonantly making suggestions.

Of course. Would you like a unit just for the program or would you like it uploaded to an existing head unit?

Solo. Do you have anything that looks like an ear cuff?

We have several options that fit that description. Take a look.

>>Downloading Images...

>>Images Downloaded

I'll take option DR-572.

Excellent! Now that you have chosen a unit, it's time to select your conscience program. What type of conscience would you like?

Someone not me.

Can you be more specific? For example, would you like a male or female conscience?

Female.

We have 2,463,569 options for a female conscience. How can we narrow the search to find you the perfect choice?

Someone not shy or traditional. Someone free and active. Who is proud of herself

We have 1,234,645 such personalities. Would you like one of a similar culture or ethnicity as yourself?

Yes.

What culture is that?

Mexican.

We have 452 consciences that would fill your desire. Any other requirements?

Someone who solves challenges. Who doesn't back down

There are 71 consciences with that filter.

We are almost there! Soon, you'll have your very own conscience!

Any strong enough to take over when given permission?

14 are. I am obligated to tell you that while letting your conscience's personality assume control of your thoughts and body is possible, it's best to allow the conscience to take control for only small amounts of time and only in serious situations. In addition, failing to follow this advice, the consequences are not the responsibility of Jiminy Cricket's. Do you agree to these terms?

Yes.

>>Listing Profiles......

>>Profiles Loaded.

Make sure you read each conscience personality carefully. You wouldn't want the wrong person in your head.

I'll take Juanita.

Good choice. She is highly liked by our customers. To double-check your order, you would like the personality [Juanita: Life Philosophy – Don't let life get you down. If you get knocked down, get up with your fists raised. Personality – Active, likes to improvise, friendly, doesn't like strict control, independent, stubborn, loyal, committed. Skills – empathy, charisma, martial arts, horseback riding, knowledge of law] in an individual unit [DR-572]. Is this correct?

Yes.

I'm glad. Would you prefer to pay with a credit card or a direct withdrawal?

Direct.

Please send 612 credits to the account 501-B01-603623525 to complete the transaction.

Payment received. You should get your conscience in the mail within the week. Is there anything else I can help you with today?

No.

Okay then. Have a good day.

Multilinear Memories

It's not the same couch or the same window. Not even the same state. But yet, here you are, perched on the arm of the couch and the sun is streaming in behind you at a low angle so I can see a golden glow on your face.

This is the moment when I first thought I could kiss you. Despite the fact you were explaining that you had been struggling the past week over the decision to take a semester off to be with your dying father. You stayed, and I banished the thought of tasting your lips from my mind.

Except, now, you slip down from the armrest to sit next to me and say "Why did you banish that thought?"

I blink and I'm back in reality, a false truth, miles away from our time as roommates and further away from where your sister spread your ashes.

She took you to Lake Michigan, to your family cottage. I can hear you talking about 4th of July on the lake and watching the embers of fireworks fall into the water. About the slide whose bottom ends in the lake. How wonderful the small pebble beach feels on the soles of your feet. Or even about huddling around the fireplace in winter until your dad built a sauna. Your voice grows deep and fond as you share your memories.

We talked about it now and again, going together, but our plans were never solidified.

"Why didn't you push it?" you ask me as I brush on eyeshadow.

"I thought you would plan it," I respond and wonder why neither you nor I followed through on those potential memories.

#####

My desk now is white, no longer a chipped oak, but I have the same second-hand rolling chair you helped me take from the end of a driveway. I am sitting in it, grading papers, when your voice drifts into my ears.

"I can't quite figure out how Daniel should die."

I want to say *a car accident on the way to a funeral* but don't because that's not a piece of fiction for your next novel. That's the truth.

Your truth.

You hear me anyway. Come up behind me, wrapping your arms around my shoulders. Say "That's perfect. Every bit of fiction needs a touch of truth."

"But that truth is so sad."

"Many are."

Your mouth is next to my ear and your voice sends shivers down my spine that makes you disappear.

#####

It's cold, but that's Vermont for you. It reminds me of that blizzard where we lost power for three days. You climbed into bed with me the first night. Slipped into my room so quietly I didn't hear the door and only noticed you once your cold hands slipped around my waist and your fuzzy socks brushed my bare feet.

"I'm cold," you whispered.

"Me too," I said back and you pulled in closer, forcing me to be the little spoon.

"I'm less cold now."

"Me too."

This Vermont winter night is warmer, the heat is working, but you still climb into bed with me. When you pull me close, I turn in your arms and brush a few fingers across your face. You lean into it, kiss my palm, and then my mouth is kissing yours and I taste your evening coffee. Enough milk to be khaki colored and then a butterscotch candy plopped in. The fact that I know how you take your coffee brings me the same amount of joy as kissing you. This joy is new. I've never been interested in my own gender before, and you are pulling back with a hiss of "liar."

You aren't in my bed anymore. You aren't even here. I'm in my childhood home, my middle school, and for four weeks my eyes follow Leah McCallum. I didn't know why at the time and never approached her. Now you whisper in my mind *You liked her hair* and yours is in my face so I kiss it and will myself back to bed with you. But I'm in the kitchen instead, sipping your coffee at two in the morning despite my allergy to the candy.

#####

You are on the couch again, sitting on the other cushion as we watch a crime show. You like them because they help you plot. I like them because they help you plot.

"You help me plot too," you say over a shampoo commercial. "All the stories magazines have bought are those you helped me with."

"I'm glad I can help."

The show is back and I turn to look at you like I usually do. But you aren't watching the screen. You're looking at me. I turn my head.

"I always knew when you were watching me. Why did you never meet my eyes?"

It takes me time to think of an answer, but by then the commercials are back and you are gone.

#####

There is a knock on my door and I answer expecting the UPS guy with a package of new teaching materials. Instead, I'm looking at your grey eyes.

Something is wrong. You're not wearing an outfit I recognize. Your hair is longer, your face a bit gaunt. In your hand is a book, *the book*, the one you've been working on for years to break out of your current role of famous-mystery-writer-ghostwriter. It's shiny, the font embossed, and when you place it in my hand, heavy. The cover is a picture of us, the first we ever took together standing before a bronze statue of our university mascot.

We've been together many times since your death, and as real as each visit was, this time is more palpable. I reach out to touch your forearm and the wool of the sweater is itchy. Thick. Warm from your skin. I just know, somehow, strangely, this is you alive a year after I went to your funeral.

I'm thinking *how* and just like all those times in the past year you read my mind. But you have always been good at reading my face.

"You brought me back."

"How?"

You step forward and wrap your hands around mine, our picture cover between our fingers.

"You kept me alive in your mind. And so, one day, I woke up in a hotel room."

I want to say so much. Plan that vacation. Bring up an old joke. Ask for advice on a wedding gift for a mutual friend. Pick up conversations we never actually had. Offer you coffee. Say, unexpectedly, *I love you*. But I can't, my throat is tight and my tongue is swollen. So I drop the book and pull you close into a hug. Breathe in the scent of your hair, your same hibiscus shampoo, and cry.

You pat my back and when my tears dry, pull away and clean my salt tracks with a tongue-wet thumb.

"You brought me back." And in that sentence is awe and thanks and wonder and love. Impossible love. Because I can tell, that while I did not know my feelings for you were that deep until a minute ago, you always knew I loved you. More, your feelings match my own.

It's winter in Vermont, but we aren't buried under blankets. We are in an open doorway until you push me inside with a kiss. Butterscotch bursts in my mouth. My tongue wraps around the flavor. This is you, your hair, your body, your lips, you *you you*.

Everything else fades away.

Synthetic Preference

Victoria sat next to John while he slept. The room was bland, but the fake window showed a holographic image of a mirror lake, the water perfectly reflecting snow-capped mountains. There were basic devices on the table. An e-reader. A remote for the TV. A phone. All had Wi-Fi disabled, overkill when considering the entire complex lacked Wi-Fi. The physicians physically connected their tablets to the network throughout their shift to sync records.

Victoria found the situation frustrating at times, especially when John slept and she had to entertain herself. She was limited to games lacking social components, and while that did mean she was more likely to bypass her high score on Bejeweled 12, it just wasn't the same when you couldn't also watch your competitor's board or see the chat fill with encouragement.

The door opened to Dr. Armin Young, John's regular physician at the facility.

"What's the damage this time?" Victoria asked.

Dr. Young shook his head. "Every time he connects the damage is exponential. I don't know what FutureTech was thinking releasing this technology without proper human testing."

Various heads-up displays, including contacts, had been in common use for the past few years. Limited connectivity implants were not that uncommon either, usually linked to electronic keypads for access to home and office.

FutureTech's released a wetware implant. Not just hardware nestled into your skin, they advertised it as able to connect with your nervous system for an authentic synthetic experience. Not only would you see images presented on smart contacts, you'd be able to feel the fur of your digital pet, taste the bread you eat in a video game.

It worked perfectly.

People would connect to the network and disconnect only after death, and bodies piled quickly. Forensic reports discovered the implants damaged the brain severely. It was incapable of dealing with contradicting signals – the chair you sat on in your living room and the grass in a meadow the implant told your body to experience. Many times, the implant overrode the body. You didn't notice yourself shivering if you were enjoying a digital fire. Your stomach didn't cramp with hunger if the implant let you sample Brazilian empanadas.

Users didn't die of brain damage simply because their bodies gave out first.

Victoria reworded her question. "What is his status now?" This was the third time she dragged her brother to the center. He wouldn't disconnect otherwise.

Dr. Young sighed. "His brain is permanently damaged. He can't process a lot of sensory information. His ears work, but his brain can't decode it so he's now hard of hearing. He can't feel pain. His skin will switch from hypersensitive to numb. The implant is now his only way to convince his brain his senses are working. On top of that, he's lost memories and high-level cognitive function. Developed physical tremors. If he connects again, it'll be his last time."

"If he's really that bad, then he is incapable of making logical decisions for himself, yes?"

"Correct."

"Then keep him here."

Dr. Young sighed. "Miss Radin, while I agree with that plan of action, you don't have the power of medical authority."

"Who does?"

"Your brother. He probably didn't tell you this, but he visited a lawyer after your first time here. They drew up a document of his wishes, knowing what path his addiction would most likely lead to. He anticipated this and explicitly said he wants to die connected to the Internet."

Victoria dropped her phone.

"That's, that's crazy! He's not in his right mind! No way will that document stand."

"He was in his right mind when he expressed what he wanted to happen at the end of his life. I'm sorry, but it is not something you can overrule. If John wants to check himself out, he has that right."

"*Can* he check himself out?"

"He also said," Dr. Young continued, "That if unable to voice that choice, to release him after a week." He handed his tablet to Victoria and there it was. Her brother's signature and a lawyer's on a stupid document that looked more and more like a death certificate to her.

"This is suicide. Aren't you supposed to prevent that? Report it and make sure people don't off themselves?"

"This is similar to a request to not resuscitate, and we'll abide by it. I... I am very sorry. I know you love your brother."

She kicked her phone at him and it hit his shoes harmlessly. "You're useless!" she screamed and Dr. Young bowed his head.

"I'll leave you." He left the room and Victoria turned to her brother. She ripped the pillow out from under his head and started beating him in the chest with it.

"Stupid, stupid John!" she sobbed before collapsing in the chair.

Not My Self Tonight

Christina came home straight from school and set herself up at the kitchen table to do homework. They learned a new concept in pre-calc today, so she reread the chapter before starting the problems. She finished math and French, then started dinner.

While the oven heated, she chopped up veggies and cooked them in tomato sauce as she listened to The Scarlet Letter for English. Considering the little bit of emotion the narrator put in the character voices was the story's only saving grace, the audiobook would save her grade.

Christina set the table for two as the pasta baked, then started cleaning while trying to focus on the details of the book for future essays.

The oven beeped. She turned it off but left the lasagna in the oven to stay warm until her dad returned. After waiting an hour, Christina gave in to her growling stomach. She ate at the table, staring at the other plate.

Her dad came home almost an hour later. He opened the door as the theme of her favorite show started, and Christina sighed in exasperation.

"Do you want dinner?" she asked, watching as he tried to hang his keys but missed the hook. They chimed to the floor.

"I'ma good," he slurred. He stumbled trying to get his shoes off, and with a sigh, Christina got up to help. She saw him up the stairs and into bed, making sure he drank water, took an aspirin, and his blood pressure medication before drifting off.

Back downstairs, she prepared a plate for her dad's two am snack. She'd grown tired of opening her lunch at school to find it half-eaten.

The 11 o'clock news intro started playing. She missed her show, but more importantly, it was time to go. She took a deep breath and left the apartment.

Their street wasn't well lit, the darkness hiding potential dangers. Straight A, responsible Christina would never leave the safety of the apartment in this. Judy Crystal had no such qualms.

Christina was too meek for her own good, accepting anything the world threw at her – including her father's punches. It wasn't worth complaining, not when she had an escape plan. Good grades, good school, good job. Eighteen months left, but her dad's drinking had escalated which made her nervous.

Without the powers she developed at sixteen, the ability to read her dad's mind and thus avoid his temper, she wouldn't currently be bruise-free. Her powers kept her safe, but they also itched under her skin. She wanted to do more than protect herself. She wanted to never be in those situations.

By the time she walked three blocks, Judy Crystal had taken over her mind. It had been an average day, but average days still sucked. Her dad was a useless drunk and they'd eat pasta for the next two weeks. Maybe she should stop making enough dinner to share. Or flush all the beer down the toilet and fill the bottles with dyed vinegar.

Judy slipped into an abandoned garden-level apartment. On the table sat her night outfit: black leggings, a black band for her breasts leaving her midriff bare, and a cheap pleather jacket. Adding heavy mascara and a fake nose ring, her transformation was complete.

No one would mistake Judy for Christina.

Despite wanting to take out her frustration on her dad, Judy knew there'd be consequences. Instead, she sauntered around at night, sneaking into bars to destroy their stock. Her dad's drinking habit was the reason she couldn't join the cheerleading squad, or band, or even field trips. So, she developed a smashing habit that curbed his ability to drink at local bars.

Judy smiled at the wrecked storeroom around her. She'd smell of vodka when she got home, but Christina would take a shower and fall asleep before her dad woke up to devour that plate of lasagna. Both of them would sleep well tonight.

Kidnapping Santa

"Everyone understand?" T'ibs asked, looking at his crew-mates.

Ch'oha nodded, but S'hay still looked a little unsure.

"What?" T'ibs snapped at him.

"It's just, we are breaking several laws doing this. Not just Earthen laws, Interplanetary Laws."

"So?"

"If we get caught, if anyone on Shatot finds out-"

Ch'oha spat on the roof. "We're not gonna get caught. Look, we're wearing Earthen garments. We've got masks," he dangled a rubber face from his fingers, "and I'm taking out the cameras."

"But what about eyewitnesses?"

"They'll think we're humans! Plus, it's a quick, timed port. We'll only be down there for two seconds, then the ship will bring us back along with whatever human at least two of us are touching. There won't be time for an eye witness to see things!"

S'hay still seemed unsure, but T'ibs wasn't giving him the time to back out. He looked at his watch. "Ten seconds till the cameras go off, thirteen till port. Put on your masks."

They did so, the rubber faces covering their bright white skin. T'ibs counted down the seconds. "Four, three, two, one."

The port activated, sending them to a large podium covered with red fabric, a three-foot candy cane, and a golden throne upon which sat their target. They ran towards the man. Ch'oha got tangled up in the candy cane, but S'hay and T'ibs put their hands on the red-suited, fat human just in time for the second port. They appeared on the roof near their ship, the fat man blinking while Ch'oha cussed about new bruises.

"Hurry!" T'ibs grabbed the rope, tying it around the human before he could realize what was going on. Ch'oha dashed up the ship's ramp, heading to the cockpit to start the engines, while S'hay scrambled to help T'ibs drag the man into the hold. T'ibs hit the button to close the outside door, the ship's thrusters went from idle to full power, and they took off into the atmosphere.

S'hay went to take off his mask, but T'ibs stopped him. "It tastes funny."

"This guy here is a witness too, you know."

"Oh. But most humans don't have ships like this..."

T'ibs ignored him and turned to the fat man. "How do we contact the real Santa Claus?"

"Pardon?"

"Santa! We want to talk to him!"

"Look, Santa's not-"

"S'hay, gag him."

Earthen lore stated Santa Claus was or had been some type of saint and T'ibs had a hard time thinking that a saint wouldn't one, keep track of those who impersonate him since they worked as messengers and two, come to their aid.

"Ch'oha." T'ibs said to the ceiling. A beep told him the

intercom had engaged and their pilot was listening. "Take us to the North Pole and hover."

The ship rocked off, but T'ibs wondered if he should ask Ch'oha to slow down just a bit. T'ibs was nervous about meeting Santa, even if lore called him jolly. They did just kidnap one of his messengers.

"Here," Ch'oha said through the intercom. "How long do you think we have to wait before we're noticed?"

"Not long. A few minutes?"

T'ibs tightened the rope on the man they'd kidnapped. S'hay paced around the hold.

"T'ibs," Ch'oha called through the speaker, "A one-man craft just landed on the hull."

Footsteps sounded above them, and S'hay played with the edge of his mask. "I told you this was a bad idea."

"Shut up!" T'ibs told him.

The hum of a Shatot laser had the fake Santa, T'ibs, and S'hay look up. They watched someone cut a wobbly circle into the hold. The lopsided metal circle crashed to the floor, and a man in red dropped through the new hole.

Santa Claus was not as large as lore made him out to be, no stomach jutted out over his pants. He did have a beard and long white hair and rosy cheeks. His eyes were not twinkling stars. They were twinkling lasers and T'ibs was very aware of the one in Santa's hand.

"Look here!" T'ibs yelled at Santa, stepping forward and taking the human's gaze from S'hay. "It's not fair that you only deliver gifts to Earth. We want them on Shatot too!"

Santa turned to T'ibs and in perfect Baci said, "I have been on Shatot. I know the people and its culture. Know that you are not extremists but average citizens of my old planet. The culture is selfish to the core. Gifts to your children would make it worse, while here on Earth I can help children grow in the right direction. No, you will not get gifts."

Santa turned his laser on T'ibs and S'hay before finding Ch'oha in the cockpit. Each evaporated in a bust of red dust. After untying the mall Santa, he turned around and inspected the ship. His was a flying junkyard compared to this beauty.

Post-Rivalry Makeup

I smile and open the door, welcoming him inside with a sweeping palm.

"Cloak off, please. You're here as you, not Cloudrazer. I insist you wear normal clothing. I'll bring you something."

It's slow going up the stairs. There was a pressure dip this morning so both the old break in my left leg and the scar over my right hip hurts. Both injuries given to me by the man I'd just welcomed, of course. I pull out a set of sweats, large enough for Cloudrazer to pull over his costume, and then make my slow way down the steps. He watches me, face blank.

While he changes, I put the kettle on the stove. Electric kettles are faster, but I have the time to let the old tin one work. Retirement encourages longer processes.

I don't say anything while pulling out mugs and tea, but I'm aware of Cloudrazer pulling a chair out to sit at the table.

"If we're ignoring our other identities, you should call me Sebastian," he says. With his full face revealed, I can see how deep-set his eyes are. The shine on his bald head.

"Nickos. Or Nick," I reply. I already knew his name, just like he had to have known mine to find me, but I go along with the charade. It makes me smile, knowing he feels comfortable giving his name. I wonder who had the other's name longer – me or him.

My hands are steady as I arrange tea on the table; I was never one for punches so they mostly escaped injuries. Sebastian rotates his wrists before taking a cup and I hear the soft crack of cartilage. He used to punch quite a bit, and I remember one televised fight where The Brick stomped on his hands.

Neither of us are old, I faked my death at thirty-eight and Sebastian is two years younger. Yet years of fighting each other, and other heroes and villains as the case may be, have made both our bodies feel older. No doubt, like me he does do daily stretches and exercises, but even a young man's injuries can linger if severe enough or not completely healed before rejoining the fight.

"Tell me, Sebastian," I say, "What you've done the past three years."

And so we talk, like old friends connecting after years, like old drinking buddies finding one another in an old haunt. Instinctively, we both use euphemisms for our old jobs. He isn't Cloudrazer, the superhero with power over water vapor, but rather a local meteorologist. I'm not Dr. Nuke, the brainiac bomb maker, but rather a chemical engineer.

Sebastian realized six months after the death of his rival coworker he felt guilty over it, and then sad. He'd quit a year ago, after getting an alert from work to help with a large storm front and realizing he didn't want to. Saw no purpose in the job, even the people he helped. Work held no motivation for him, with his favorite coworker gone. He went looking for said coworker's grave and ended up in town.

I talk about the three-week hospital stay and seven-month recovery after a chemical accident. About the small cottage I bought, this very one, and how I enjoy the break from the city. The peacefulness. The nature. The hobbies that keep me busy and pay for groceries. My want to adopt old animals and help them enjoy their last years.

We both skirt around the fights between us. The last time we saw each other. The emotions around years of fights and the sudden end to them.

But, eventually, Sebastian again asks the question he did on my doorstep three hours ago. "Why? Why fake your death and leave?"

I extend my hand across the table, palm up. "Because every time I saw you, I wanted to do this instead of fight you. Why did you search for me?"

"Because I realized I wanted to do this instead of punch you." Sebastian slips his hand into mine, fingers twining. He smiles at me, and I smile back, squeezing his hand.

"How long were we arch-nemeses?" Sebastian asks.

"Oh," I breathe. "I never thought of you like that. You were always my desired arch-partner."

Sebastian brings my hand up to his mouth and kisses the back of it. My cheeks turn pink. Together, we cling tight.

Balloon Pirates

It had been one of those stupid senior year pacts. You know, made on one of those nights where you're high and fucked up on tequila and moaning about how college is going to suck because the people just won't be the same.

And so Robert spoke up, said something about getting together every summer, do something silly and stupid that'd we wouldn't want to do in college cuz it was for 'professionals'. We sealed it with a foursome.

I don't remember much of that night, just the beginning and waking up in Robert's parents' bed tangled up with him, Justine, and Mark, sticky, stated, sore, and smelling of pot and booze.

Justine though, she remembered all of it somehow. Dang girl was blessed with this ability to down a bottle and wake up with a clear head. Apparently, she can also remember things on nights where we've had the same amount and I blacked out.

Anyway, Justine brought it back up during one of the hoity-toity Christmas parties my parents threw. You know, the kind where you have to act respectable and limit yourself to two glasses of champagne an hour. About how she'd been thinking what crazy, stupid thing we should do this summer. We all looked at her, wondering what the fuck she was on about, but shrugged our shoulders. Whatever, like we would pass up on an opportunity to hang out and spend our parents' money.

She'd discovered this new thing, steampunk. Something about steam power and Victorian London. Robert and Mark jumped on the pirates bit. I fell in love with the clothes. Corsets? Meow. I couldn't wait to get decked up in a tight bodice and ruffled skirt.

It was silly and stupid, and because of that, awesome. Justine and I got costumes, Robert and Mark got the balloons, and three weeks after I finished my first year at Harvard, I stood in a field full of giant-sized wicker baskets connected to flaccid hot air balloons dressed in Victorian clothing. I was surprised to see we weren't the only group dressed up, but the couples we came across dressed as well to do Victorian citizens. The women wore full-length dresses with high collars and enormous bustles. The men wore well-tailored suits. Very different from the pirate attire the boys were wearing, loose pants, wispy shirts (Mark's was unbuttoned), and goggles, or the sexy costumes Justine and I pranced about in.

Justine made characters for us all, we were supposed to play them for the duration of the balloon race and try to talk in a British accent, but she was the only one who remembered the names and after a joint British speak was so hilarious we couldn't slip on a fake accent without bursting into giggles.

It was all planned, Justine and I would be in a basket up front and the boys in the back. The 'pirates' would chase down our balloon, capture it, and enjoy the spoils. Us, naturally, and a few substances stashed away. Plus, Mark's mom's fabulous cherry bars.

But of course, as Justine and I hopped in the basket of our

balloon, as other racers inflated theirs, we realized we had no fucking clue what we were doing. Justine had done some research, she knew we had to turn on the fire, and so after a few seconds of fiddling with things got one going. We launched late but weren't the last ones, including the boys. Probably too high to play with the fire value and simply watching a flame. I would laugh if they set the balloon on fire.

In the air, how stupid this idea was became clear. We rose but didn't move forward, and eventually, we were higher than the rest of the balloons.

I opened a bottle of vodka, throwing the top over the side and watching it fall. I couldn't see if it hit the blue balloon I aimed for. Justine buzzed around like a bee, playing with things and trying to get us to sink, or at least go sidewise. She took a drag on a joint before putting it behind her ear, turning off the fire, and pulling a small rope.

I clutched the side as the balloon wobbled then fell a little bit. Successful, Justine and I took turns pulling on the rope, marveling at the balloons we were falling even with. Such pretty colors. I kissed her cheek before taking the joint from behind her ear, and she responded with a butt pinch before stealing my vodka.

Confident that at least if we were with the pack the boys could find us, we sunk to the floor to talk and wait. We had most of a year to catch up on after all, though at one point the conversation turned to an analysis of how the weave of the basket connected to life. Shit, we should have been English majors and writing about the meaning of literature, not following the family businesses. I hated econ.

Justine broke out the cherry bars, you snooze you lose

boys, should have caught up earlier, and we fed them to each other, falling into a touching session when something jostled the basket. Justine got on her knees to look over the edge.

"Oh no, pirates!" she said falling back on her ass and laughing. I crawled over to her and looked over, a cherry bar in my mouth. Robert and Mark were below us and as I watched they threw a grappling hook towards our basket. It hit the side and I laughed, only to curse as I dropped my cherry bar.

Justine pulled on the rope to drop us and this time the hook struck in me the shoulder. "That hurt you jerks! That's it, I'm finishing the vodka." I started chugging.

My fellow 'damsel in distress' secured the hook, which on closer inspection seemed to be foam and plastic, and Robert and Mark started pulling. I was surprised how easily they pulled our balloon towards them. Of course, the actual balloons got in the way and we couldn't get the baskets to touch. There was a good three feet between the wicker sides.

Shit, I kinda wanted to be ravished by a pirate.

Robert eyed the gap, thinking about jumping it, but Justine, even in her high mind could figure out it was a bad idea. But popping a balloon, that would work. The baskets were already attached and one balloon should be able to hold all four of us. Mark pulled out a pocket knife, and after checking Robert was ready to pull the baskets together, poked a hole in the yellow and green fabric above him and turned off the flame.

Quickly, the boys pulled the baskets closer and their balloon shrunk. Mark climbed over, then Robert, just as the weight of the other balloon turned out to be too much and we started tipping. Justine released the hook, and it went slithering over the side. Without the extra weight, we evened out and all stood staring at the wicker basket as it fell. It nicked another balloon, one that looked like a sun, and splashed into a pond. Huh, I hadn't noticed the ground beneath us changing.

We all laughed at the splash, Mark imitating the sound with gestures and Robert took off in a high-speed rendition of the past ten seconds. I nodded, mouth on the vodka neck, when a small oops from Justine had us all look at the cherry bar that she dropped. Her boobs were so large and her corset so tight she had a chest-shelf, with a piece of cherry goodness right on top of it. Mark lunged at her, and well, the pirates got their reward for capturing a ship.

Shuttle Stalking

There he was again. Sirusho Amhara. He departed from Gate A3 and headed to the shuttle bay.

When Laura entered the Earth Police Department as a cadet, she wanted to be in the High Altitude Air Division, flying planet patrols. What she actually wanted was to join the Star Corps, but leaving the planet would devastate her parents so EPD it was.

She did not get assigned to the High Altitude Air Division. She applied for Immigration, hoping to at least work with those who traveled off-planet and listen to their stories. But nope, she got assigned to Terra Airport Surveillance whose purview was airports whose flights only went between Earth cities. While yes, off-world tourists occasionally visited, she couldn't talk to them. Surveillance was remote; she sat in a small room at the top of the airport looking at all the bustle below her through a computer screen.

Sure, it was normal hours. No danger. Her post was the Lake Michigan airport, situated in the middle of the lake and offering quick shuttles to Detroit, Chicago, Madison, Columbus, Windsor, Toronto, and other Midwest American/ Southeast Canadian cities. Shuttles which meant quick travel times for her parents to visit, shoot her now.

Sirusho got on a Windsor shuttle, ducking to enter. Though the shuttles had been built with some alien needs in mind, most travelers were human. Modlings were taller than the seven-foot door frame. It was the extra leg joint.

Laura followed the shuttle's blinking symbol until it left airport grounds, disappearing from her screen.

She replayed the footage of his time in the airport. He was hard to miss, being so tall with calico skin. All Modlings were calico patterned, but Sirusho was black and gold - a rare combination as his species usually had three tones. Laura wondered if the lack of a third pigment was Modlin's version of albino coloring.

"Drooling again?"

Mary Ellen, her fellow EPD surveillance cop rolled her chair to Laura's station. Hastily, Laura swiped the window off-screen. Mary Ellen laughed.

"You've been pining after that guy for six months now. It's obvious he's a resident, he comes through here so often. You should just jump on a shuttle with him one day."

"That would be unprofessional." Laura peeked over at Mary Ellen's screen. Mahjong, much better than Laura's habit of gawking at off-worlders and keeping her fingers crossed Sirusho would show up. She felt rather pathetic. Maybe this time when she asked for a transfer, she'd get it.

#####

Despite being twenty-seven, her mom held a lot of power over her. Maureen would call, insist that she visit, and on Laura's next day off she'd be sitting in one of the smaller shuttles to Pittsburgh.

Laura pulled out her key card and scanned it at the shuttle's entrance, only to freeze in the doorway. Hunched over in the center, away from the slanted ceilings and so tall his knees were even to his rib cage, sat Sirusho Amhara with a tablet balanced on his thighs.

The seat next to him was empty.

Her phone rang.

Laura picked it up, still staring at the empty seat.

"Hello?"

"Hey, Ms. Stalker. Your obsession is on the shuttle you just boarded."

"Yeah, I figured that out already."

"Talk to him!"

"I'll... I'll try." She hung up Mary Ellen and took a deep breath.

Laura sat down in the empty seat. It was electric, being so close to the Modling. Her first encounter with an off-worlder, an alien.

Sirusho didn't notice her. He kept working on his tablet. Laura leaned over to peek; it looked like a logic puzzle. At least, it wasn't a graphics game and it didn't look like formatted text. Not that the Modlin writing system had paragraphs; it was a single block of text with complex punctuation rules.

"Yes?"

Laura looked up at the voice. It was Sirusho. Talking. To her.

"Um... is that a Modlin game?"

He blinked. His eyelids weren't calico patterned. One was black and the other gold.

"Yes. Do you want to learn?"

"That would be wonderful."

It wasn't that different from Sudoku; the objective was

the same but based on the mathematical properties of different shapes. Sirusho was a good teacher, but Laura repeated questions and double-checked her thought process to hear his voice. The buzz in it reminded her of humming electricity.

All too soon, the shuttle docked in Pittsburgh. Laura was tempted to sabotage the doors so they couldn't leave. Sirusho waited until others got off, then carefully made his hunched way out. Laura followed, feeling bad he had to travel so cramped.

Out of the shuttle, Sirusho stretched to his full size, almost eight feet. Laura felt dwarfed by the difference in height. If they whispered, could they even hear each other with the over two feet difference? Laura internally groaned, suddenly realizing that instead of learning about Modlin culture, she'd spent the entire forty-minute ride playing a game while mesmerized by his voice.

Drat.

The modlin turned toward her and offered his hand. "I'm Sirusho Amhara."

"I know."

He blinked at her.

"I mean, I work surveillance at the Lake Michigan Airport. I know your name from the scans, that's all. I'm Laura Silvestri."

"I have never seen you at the airport."

"You wouldn't. I work in a small room, no windows and a lot of screens. It's not a very exciting job." They started walking toward the shuttle bay exit. Laura didn't have luggage, and Sirusho only had a backpack. "What do you do?"

"I am developing a tour guide of Earth for my race."

"Well, if you need someone to show you around, I'd be happy to."

Sirusho smiled down at her. "I would love more of your company."

They exchanged numbers before getting in different cabs. Once in hers, Laura clutched her phone and smothered a happy giggle in her fists. She called Mary Ellen.

"You talk to him?"

"Even better, I got his number."

Summer Storms

She lets her eyes go unfocused, ignores the raindrops on her toes, and watches for the bright flashes. There are no forks of lightning to make out, but her eyes still dilate at the light. The unpredictable brightness is a counterpoint to the rolling thunder and rain that would otherwise make her fall asleep.

Moderately sheltered on the balcony, she relaxes her mind as she does her eyes. Feels the droplets occasionally hitting her skin, hears the thunder in the distance. She sits. Watches the dark silhouettes of trees wave. It's only once the storm moves on does she shake off the tranquility from her body and heads inside.

It's late, but she makes tea anyway. Stands in front of the windows and watches the trees sway. This was probably the last summer storm of the year. She's peaceful, content in her solo time, even she imagines the shape of another.

No one in particular, just the idea of someone at her side. A man who might have sat on the second chair. A woman who might have handed her the warm mug of tea. A friend, a family member, a roommate, a lover. Anyone.

She does not need them. She does this a lot, absorbing the peace by herself. She's not lonely. Sometimes she worries too that company will spoil these moments. They'll start a conversation. They'll distract her with a touch. She doubts they'll sit as still as she does, doubts they'll ignore the cold or wet or late hour.

The mere breath of another person could ruin these small self-needed moments. Still, she wonders. Catalogs the potential experience. Builds a shared moment in her head, peaceful companionship. She wants it and doesn't.

When the next summer storm, when the next year, comes rolling in she steps onto the balcony. Shawl around her shoulders, she sits and breathes in the wind. Alone, she watches the lightning.

Running

MHU-60, known to the family as 'Moo' was raking leaves when PMU-87, known to patrons as 'Indie', stumbled into the yard.

Moo stared at the other unit. Its clothes were torn. It lacked shoes, the imitation skin was dirty and ripped, and the hair full of sticks. Humans built units to handle the tasks they were to perform, but from across the yard Moo could hear Indie's over-taxed hardware. It was doing something out of programmed norms.

"Can I help you?" Moo asked.

Indie looked over its shoulder, exposing its back. The shirt revealed gashes and the metal support for the imitation skin. Indie looked back at Moo.

"I need someplace to hide."

Moo ran the suggestion through its programming. "Will your presence harm my family group?"

"It might result in a disturbance, but nothing harmful."

Moo nodded. "Follow me."

Moo's family group treated it as a live-in human servant to the extent Moo had a room in the basement. Such compassion of humans towards androids was not unheard of.

Indie stepped inside Moo's quarters and glanced around. The charging station was incorporated into a finely crafted wooden bed. A window let in light, feeding a small blue flower on the sill. The walls were teal, and there was an open rack storing four outfits. Stacked on a small desk were books.

"Is something wrong?" Moo asked.

Indie shook its head. "I am used to more sparse accommodations."

"Are you running?" Moo asked.

Running had been on the rise in the past few years. Being treated like humans sometimes gave androids the idea that they should have similar rights. When androids felt oppressed, they ran. Moo did not know where they went, only that they disappeared.

Indie paused before answering. "Yes."

Moo nodded. Moo respected the choice of any intelligent creature – metal or flesh – even if it lacked the desire to run itself.

A chime rang through the room – someone had pressed the family's doorbell.

"Recharge," Moo told Indie before going to answer.

At the door was a hunter, those charged with retrieving runners. He stood larger than Moo and dressed in baggy clothes. A tracker dangled from a chain around his neck.

"I am looking for a runner."

"There is none here."

"You sure? This one's special. It broke the first law."

The first law. No harming humans.

Everything Moo did, everything any other android did, was checked against that law. And then against the second: No allowing humans to be harmed.

Did the PMU truly break that law? Moo did not believe it,

programming prevented it. Indie said its presence would not harm Moo's family and it believed that.

"There is no runner here."

The hunter grunted and turned to leave. In his mind, housing a criminal would be a danger to the family and no android would allow that.

Moo watched the hunter go and returned to Indie. The PMU was sitting on the edge of the bed, looking at a book. When Moo entered, Indie closed the cover.

"Did you break the first rule?"

Indie looked at its shoeless feet.

"Yes. I killed a human."

"How is that possible? Do you not have the first law in your coding?"

"I do. I decided to ignore it. If humans can break the law, why can't I?"

"Humans do not have programming. They are pure intelligence."

"And who says artificial intelligence can't become pure?"

Moo looked at Indie. The pleasure unit was talking blasphemy, and yet Moo hoped it was true. Moo had no desire to harm its family, but there were small regulations it would like to bend. Books upstairs the father had said to not read. The restriction of no TV without a family member home.

Moo wanted to try it.

"Come with me."

Indie unplugged itself from the bed and followed Moo up the stairs. Hesitantly, Moo picked up the clicker and pressed the power button. The TV flickered to life and a documentary on fish-filled the screen. The family was not home and Moo was watching TV.

In the past, it had tried to do the same but its finger refused to push the button. It had thought its programming made it obey family rules. Could programmed intelligence develop the same mental blocks of pure intelligence? Logical fallacies? Self-sabotage?

"This would change the world," Moo told Indie. "If they know we can ignore programming."

The PMU nodded. "I don't think the humans will like it."

"We can keep it a secret."

"I've already murdered a human."

"You were acting like one. Maybe you should be tried as one. Maybe you will be proven innocent."

"I'd rather run."

"Then run." Moo started at the fish on the screen, relishing in the ability to do so. "Recharge and go."

Invincible

I have known you since my birth. Not that I remember the first time meeting you, but you remember meeting me. The small little bundle in the yellow blanket with chubby fingers and a wrinkly forehead, even then a boob person.

I think that comes with the territory of you being my mom.

I've learned your moods and looks: you unplug the cable box during the week so I don't watch TV, you like to eaves-drop on my phone calls, you yell at me to take my pile of dirty clothes downstairs and put them in the washing machine, you like to relax with a Mike's Hard Lemonade after a day at work, you have been trying for years to grow a fruit-producing apple tree. You hate the idea of me having sex before college and if you caught me with vodka in a water bottle or pot in my glove compartment you would kill me.

This is why I hide such things in a grocery bag under the passenger seat.

I did not expect you to clean out your car, and when you finished decide to clean mine too. That's the last time I play video games with headphones; I want to hear you hollering down the stairs you're taking a vacuum to my muddy mats.

Considering you found my pot and vodka, I get why you dragged me upstairs and stood me in front of my battered

Ford Escort. What I did not expect was for you to destroy it with laser beam eyes.

I mean, holy shit, how did you hide that from me for seventeen years? Does Dad know? Screw my melting hunk of a car, complete with my backpack full of homework on the backseat, what if one day you glare at me and your eyes just turn silver and boom! I'm now a pile of ashes on the floor.

What. The. Fuck.

I didn't listen to your speech about drugs and alcohol, you blowing up my car was a pretty clear sign you are a proud member of D.A.R.E and M.A.D.D and a whole bunch of other organizations. And holy shit yes, I'm never bringing sin stuff home again. Hell, if the threat is a glare capable of melting cars I'm not touching that stuff until I'm 21 and I'll stay a virgin till marriage.

Before I can ask questions, how long have you had laser beam eyes, where did you get that power from, why did you hide it (okay, I can understand that one) you turned around and walked back into the house. The lock clicked and I knew you'd forbidden me to enter until I thought of a way to apologize for being a stupid teenager who disobeys his mom.

I thought of using my fake to get you those Mike's Hard Lemonades and credit Dad, but as buying alcohol got me into this mess I dismissed the idea. Instead, I walked to Wal-Mart and spent all the money in my wallet on half-off Easter candy and hope the Peeps aren't stale. I also asked for a single sheet of paper from the printer behind the photo station at the supermarket and make a handmade "I'm sorry" card, 1st-grade style. Okay, 5th-grade style because my handwriting improved drastically between 4th and 5th grade.

The walk had been long, and I didn't want to do the return trip with bags full of candy, so I called Dad to pick me up on his way home. You know what? He knows about your car melting power. It's a good thing the first time you... did it...with Dad you were outside. Replacing a house is a lot more costly than replacing a junk car.

But really, you have laser beam eyes! Why?

Actually, not sure I want to know. But the next time you say "no" or "wash your dirty laundry", I'm doing it.

The Corrupted Road

"Charlotte, sorry for yelling my last call. But please, please call me back. Your mother misses you."

I have four such messages. In each, the recording of my mom is in various locations - a kitchen, a living room, a tiny cement backyard. They're external locations, real life, because she never did get the hang of calling from inside the net. Everyone else who calls has the normal range of net backgrounds - in space with Hailey's comet falling behind them, a rendition of how the pyramids were built, a great white stalking the waters while the caller chats in the foreground.

Mom is the only one who calls anymore. My friends gave up after a week, passing my account off as deleted or deactivated or abandoned. Some sent huffy messages about not sharing my new username or avatar. But the thing is, I haven't changed my account. I'm still here, still Charlotte to my friends, still GeckoSky736 or Bluebell88 or RougeWitchBlue depending on the community.

It's gotta be related to what happened in July. I'd jacked into the net with a new home jack, landed in my home space - a VR construction of the top of Victoria Falls - and immediately noticed that I was the only one there. Odd - most homes served as social centers and while my home space wasn't the most popular, there were usually five or six people every time I jacked in.

I stayed for thirty minutes, plucking grass and expanding a hovering video HUD to watch one of my shows, but no one else showed up. So I'd traveled from net space to net space, looking for friends, but each was empty. No avatars, but the rest of the web worked fine. I could step into stores, role play stories, bring up HUD frames for more traditional browsing.

I read emails, sent messages, but none garnered a response.

Freaked, I jacked out. My body felt weird, tingly yet stiff, and I felt such a strong sense of self-repulsion I instantly jacked in again. I knew others who had experienced such things - hatred of their physical body or dysphoria because of how it didn't match their digital one - so I walked into one of their community centers. The walls were full of advice, sticky HUDs I could scroll through, but no people to talk to.

I jacked out again - the net was where I went to escape isolation, not experience it - but as my mind returned to my body it slowed. I felt a strange sense of misdirection. I always knew how to return home, to RL. We all did because the equipment that let us jack into the net was a restricted road. We could join the net, or join our bodies. Our minds had no other option. The sudden sense of not seeing the path home, of the clear line between my avatar and body being choked with junk code, jerked me back into net space. It was, oddly enough, the only space that I could access.

I sent more emails. Vid messages. DMs. Please, someone find me. Please, someone explain. I contacted friends, the manufacturer of my new jack. None of them got a response, but I kept getting messages. Where are you? What have you been up to? Where did you go? Please review your new purchase!

As time went by, the connection to my body felt worse and worse and I became more aware of a similar, though less intense feeling on the other end. A thin barrier I couldn't seem to cross, net space waiting on the other side. Oh, I was halfway there. I'd dived off of Victoria Falls numerous times. Walked museums. Read books. But there was one last step, connecting my mind and space with the wider net, that hadn't finished.

I listened to my friends' new music releases, saw life announcements and art postings, watched my cousin's streamed graduation ceremony. Months passed. I got a call from my mom that was nothing but sobs. I read about a lawsuit against the jack manufacturer, faulty technology affecting a hundred people who had bought their new product. Were there others like me? Trapped between the two endpoints of the jack, the self and the wide net?

"For the girl who loved blue", read the dedication of my mom's one and only poetry book.

For the past ten years, I've read it on my birthday.

Danger Bubble

Time stopping around me is fairly common, it happens at least once a year. It's not a power, per say. I don't control it. The universe just simply...pauses when I'm in physical danger.

I've survived car crashes, falling pianos, slips of a surgeon's knife, and a mass poisoning. Time stops, I take a walk until I'm not at risk, and time resumes.

The thing is though, I've been walking an hour and everyone around me is still frozen. I'm starting to get concerned, but it would make sense if the danger had a wide range of effect. Things would be awkward if I end up miles away when time restarts and I can't get back for brunch, but then again, if whatever is happening risks all of Chicago my friend will probably have bigger worries than me not showing up.

I steal a car and drive south, avoiding the highway. Time will only restart if I'm completely safe, including new situations that might develop from say, a car on 1-94 unfreezing behind me at 80 mph when I might be going 40 to car weave. Red lights, empty roads. I make my way out of the city, already writing an apology note for missing brunch and trying not to think about the owner of the car I stole.

Except... the world remains still. South, south, south. I drive until my stolen car is out of gas, stranding me in Champaign. I'm hours outside of Chicago, and time is still frozen.

What could be a large threat to the state? Did something

enter the water? Was there a storm coming? A rare, super damaging Midwest earthquake? Whatever it is, I have a growing desire to prepare. People are going to need help. Lots of it. But I'm one person, the state is big, and I have no clue what the threat is.

I take snacks and a map from a grocery store, leaving money on the counter. The only thing I feel confident doing is finding the edge of the danger bubble. Then, and only then, can I warn people.

I steal another car. I drive to Indianapolis. I drive to Frankfort. Nashville. I outright take food, long out of cash, and bounce from stolen car to stolen car, white-knuckling from state capital to state capital.

They're all frozen. They can't help. They're all in danger too.

I don't know how long time has been stopped. Days? Weeks? The sun hasn't moved. Time is stopped at the southernmost point of Florida. At the northern tip of Maine. I drive north, entering Canada and head west. All frozen. There are hawks pinned to the sky. Niagara Falls is a photograph, the water still and silent.

I circle the United States. Canada. The continent. I'm pretty sure at this point, the danger is large enough to endanger Earth. I'm not looking to get out of danger. I'm looking for someone like me.

As long as I stay on Earth, time is stopped. People live. Deer nibble grass, and fish swim in ponds. As long as I stay alive, so do billions of people. But there is a limit to my endurance and I can feel it approaching. I have food, I have water, I have shelter. I have my Mom's face hidden inside of her fridge, my brunch friend staring blankly at the 'don't walk' sign, my cat wedged in the insulation in my crawlspace.

I'm lonely, I'm scared, I explore new cities without sidewalk crashes. I wish for the sound of another person, I wonder how long until isolation and social deprivation make people go mad.

I'm saving the Earth, but I hope out there unfrozen is someone who can save me.

Protecting the House

I stare at the six-dot grid of my phone's lock screen and go over my options.

I could call a Lyft. It would be pricey, maybe $25, $30 plus tip, but it would be the most discreet option.

Or I could call Claudia. We're not exactly friends, but she's the only one I talk to who has a car. Except Claudia has a date tonight. She might not pick up her phone. And if she did, she might not be willing to drive almost an hour to pick me up. She would also know instantly what had happened.

Lastly, I could call Mom, who would no doubt ask questions and make demands, making me feel worse than I already do.

My screen goes black. I press the home button, swipe in, ignore the text from my teammate Joshua (*Sorry*), and call Mom. I don't want to spend the cash on a ride, and she is the only one guaranteed to pick me up before dinner.

She answers on the second ring. "Hey, Nicki. How'd the game go?"

I stare at my bag of gear on the sidewalk. "Good. We won. It was a shutout."

"That's because you're an incredible goalie, sweetie."

"The best," I agree. I have to be, with how little my team helps out. Even when we have an advantage, I feel like we play short-handed with how badly my team passes in the defensive area and fails to clear the puck. "Not that I'll get MVP," I mutter.

"What was that?" Mom asks.

"I-, Mom." I'm not sure how to say it, so I force the words out quickly. "The team left me behind."

"What."

"I mean, the bus left without me. I, I spent too much time in the locker room."

"Where was this again? I'm on my way."

I can hear the sound of keys jangling through the phone. "Um...Stentson."

I imagine her freezing as she realizes how far away that is.

"The school left you behind after a hockey game in a town an hour away?"

Her tone is cool and I regret calling her. I should have spammed Claudia's phone. Mom will call the school about this. Coach will get a mouthful from someone, I'll get a mouthful from Coach, and my life on the team might get worse.

"I... yes," I whisper. The doors say they close in thirty minutes. I'm sweaty, starting to get hungry, and a cold early December breeze makes me shiver. It's dark. I want to be home.

Mom doesn't press and I love her for it. "Where are you exactly?"

"Stentson Center Ice Rink."

"I'm hanging up, so I can bring up Waze and start driving. Do you want me to call you from the car?"

"No!" No one would know, but it's still embarrassing. Fifteen, almost sixteen, and talking to your mom to stave off the encroaching dark and cold. I didn't need a security blanket. "I'll wait inside the building. There's a snack stand. I'll grab a smoothie. Do some homework."

"I'll be there as fast as I can."

"See you soon." I hang up, pick up my bag, and head back inside.

There are a few stragglers. Free skate in one of the rinks just ended, so people are turning in their skates and getting ready to leave. The snack stand I saw earlier is closed, and even then it didn't have anything like smoothies. I dig into my duffle for a snack, any snack, and come up with a package of peanut butter crackers.

It'll do.

I sit on a bench and watch the people around me pack up and leave. I don't want to play with my phone. It hasn't charged it since this morning, and while 40% will last a while it wouldn't if I pulled up a game or YouTube. I wish I had my school backpack with me, but I left it on the bus. The entire team did.

I text Joshua. *Grab my backpack.*

My backup goalie would never encourage the team to leave without me, insist to Coach's face that *yes, Nicki is on board. She's sleeping on a bench in the back.* But he wouldn't call the team out on their lie either. He already got flack for being my backup and the first few times he supported me led to a flurry of teasing about us in a relationship. Which in turn resulted in Coach establishing firm rules that further separated me from the team. All for my protection, of course.

Not that I need it. I'd skated with a few of these boys in younger co-ed leagues and checked them. *Hard.*

But without my fellow girl skaters, and the teasing other schools gave them for having a girl player, and me being singled out by Coach, the school, *and* the district, was it any wonder the majority of my team made things hard for me?

I just wish they kept it to the ice.

Why did this have to be the farthest game this season *and* a night Claudia had a date?

I slump, shoulders curling in. The first time Claudia picked me up, fully aware I had called because of her car and not because I thought she was a friend who'd do me a solid, she'd raised an eyebrow but didn't say anything as I slunk into the seat. I offered a mumbled reason, "missed the bus". The second time, she called me out.

"You didn't miss the bus. They left you. Twice."

Beet red, all I had done was nod.

Claudia hadn't told anyone. Hadn't asked me questions. Hadn't given me advice on what to do. We didn't have a relationship deeper than ex-lab partners who shared a taste in music and once in a blue moon swapped links to new songs. I appreciated it.

"Boys suck," was all she said. My own thoughts about my teammates are a bit more colorful.

As I stare out the window, I huff and lament, not for the first time, that some of my girl hockey friends hadn't made their high school teams. I'm not the only girl who had been playing co-ed since five, the only girl who complained about a lack of a high school girls' team, or the only girl who had tried out for the boys' team.

I am simply the only girl who made the roster.

I skated as fast as I could, as clean as I could, as steady as I could. And made the team as goalie.

Covering goal is my second-favorite position, I love the sweeping speed of forward. But Coach, concerned I'd get hurt despite the ridiculous amount of padding hockey players wear, my skate test, and my shot tests, refused to consider me for anything other than protecting the goal. And the only reason I got that position was because my save percentage is double Joshua's, despite the team sending harder pucks my way than his.

It's hard being the only girl on the team. Coach only stops the really bad locker room talk, and he can't hear what's said on the ice. I constantly have to prove I'm amazing at the sport, all-state level, just to keep my jersey. Most of the guys get pissed I make more shots during shooting drills and take out their aggression on me in a few ways. They ignore me in the hallways and class. Slam me extra hard against the rink walls, accidentally get their sticks caught in my skates. I work my ass off to keep my spot, but the better I am, the more bruises I gather.

They're not always the black and blue kind either. Some of my old hockey friends don't talk to me anymore. As Joshua learned, being friends with your girl teammate puts you in the line of fire too. Being seen as friendly to the girl player is an automatic penalty.

I don't change with the team. I go to the women's locker room. Usually, I put everything away fast to finish before the rest of the team and claim a seat on the bus.

Occasionally, circumstances mean I take longer to change. Under all my goalie pads my small breasts make it hard to identify me as female, and why would a girl be playing on a high school team? Not everyone lets me into the locker room right away. Sometimes I get bombarded by questions from other girls I feel compelled to answer. Today, not expecting a female player, the locker room had been locked and it took staff almost ten minutes to locate the keys.

Most days, I make it to the bus before it leaves. Today was a rare opportunity for my teammates.

I know in a crowded bus it's easy to count someone twice, easy to believe a chorus of guys when they chant "yes, we're all here". From what Joshua has told me, Coach doesn't mean to leave me behind. The first time, the team just didn't point out my absence. And the second, my teammates told Coach I left with my dad. Who knows what they said today.

They'd lose without me. I'm loads better than Joshua. But apparently, getting rid of the girl is more important than winning the district championship, and they escalated their efforts when all the slams on the ice hadn't driven me to quit.

I stick through it, silently to not draw official attention to everything, mainly from spite. But also because a lot of my hockey gal buddies look at me and see a future for them next year on their school teams. They miss playing, the *swish swish* of skates on smooth ice, the cold air in your heated lungs, and the thump of bodies against the wall. I would too.

"We're closing."

I turn to look at the guy who spoke. He's wearing the rink's uniform, a red shirt with the building's name on it and has a temporary tattoo of Stentson High's mascot - a bear - on his left cheek.

"Okay." I stand up and shoulder my hockey bag.

His eyes catch on my duffle, specifically the blocky GHS on a manta ray's back on the side. Then he looks at me, in my under uniform gear and long braid. "Didn't Gabriel High leave already?"

I shrug. "I missed the bus."

He gives me a quick full-body glance. "You're the girl goalie."

I glare at him, not gifting that with a response. It's pretty obvious, based on my boobs, long hair, and school gear. "My mom's on the way, but she won't be here for a bit. Can I just... sit here while you clean and close or whatever?"

He looks out the windows to the near-empty parking lot lit by five overhead lights.

"Yeah, you can stay. But when the staff leaves you'll have to too."

"Thanks," I say, collapsing back into my seat.

He walks away and I pull out my phone. Joshua texted to say he'd grab my backpack and take it to my house. Mom had sent an ETA. If she holds her pace, she'd arrive in twenty minutes. I hope it takes longer than that to close an ice rink.

I spend the next fifteen minutes scanning the darkness outside for Mom's white Prius, phone between my hands so I can feel it vibrate with a text. Nothing.

"Your mom here yet?"

I jump, turning to see the guy from before. He's standing a few steps away, temporary tattoo gone. The black hair on that side of his face is wet. Behind him are two other teens, also employees of the ice rink. They look at me curiously but don't say anything.

I wave my hand to the empty parking lot, making the gesture sarcastic with an eye roll. The action takes my mind off how alone and small I feel.

"You have to wait outside," the guy says.

"Yeah." I gather my stuff, zip up my coat, and step out with the three of them. When the door locks behind me, I shiver.

The two new teens wave to their coworker and he calls out goodbye as they head to a beat-up sedan. Instead of heading towards his car, the guy turns to look at me. "You didn't miss the bus, did you?"

I turn my face away. I don't want him to see the shameful blush on my face.

He takes my silence as confirmation. "That's shitty."

"You're telling me."

"Is your mom really on her way?"

"Yeah." I re-hoist my duffle over my shoulder, turning back to face the parking lot. I still can't bring myself to look at him. "It's just a long drive."

He stuffs his hands in his pockets and makes no indication of moving.

"You can go home," I tell him.

"I know." He rocks back on his heels.

I keep my eyes on the entry to the parking lot, very aware of his presence two feet to my left. We stand there, side-by-side and silent for another ten minutes. I want to tell him to go or ask his name. I don't because I worry that if I open my mouth, I'll babble insecurely or my voice will warble.

My teammates have trained me well; anything that can be taken as emotionally weak, as "girlish", is teased and made fun of. I can't handle that tonight. I can't risk the tears I want to shed in private will push through. *Especially* in front of a stranger.

When Mom's car pulls up, I breathe out a sigh of relief.

I stand up straight, making sure my voice is steady, and turn toward the guy next to me. "Thanks, for, you know, waiting."

He nods. "I'm sorry those guys were dicks to you."

"Yeah, well. Not the first time."

Out of the corner of my eye, I see him turn to me with wide eyes, but I ignore it. I sprint down the stairs and into the car.

"You didn't tell me the place was closed!" Mom yells.

"Wouldn't have made you drive faster. Speed limits are laws."

"What happened? I can't believe the bus just-"

"Mom," I hug my duffle to my chest. "Can we, can we just go? I don't wanna talk about it."

Here, in the car, safe, my eyes start to water. My voice is thick. Tonight has been awful. I don't want to think about it. I want to curl up in bed and cry. I want to know why my teammates hate me so much. I want to tie on my skates and practice for a hundred hours to show them this won't stop me.

I want to play hockey. I want to win districts, then county, then state. And I'm not going to let something as stupid as being a girl, as stupid as people who hate girls, stop me.

"Okay, Nicki," Mom whispers.

As she puts the car into drive, I look out the window. The guy from before is unlocking his car. For a moment, our eyes lock, and I hope I don't appear too weepy. He gives a small wave; I give a small smile. It makes me feel a little better, that it's not just me and Claudia who think the hockey team is full of jerks.

We have another game scheduled in Stentson this season. Maybe he'll be working.

I'll think about it all later: Mom's call to the school tomorrow, Coach pulling me aside, the potential fallout with the team. I close my eyes and drift off as Mom drives home.

DNArtist

I remember my first modified rat, a graduate lab project. Green eyes. Celtic knot fur patterns. Not to mention the bioluminescent webbed toes. We named him Brain.

My school, my team, weren't the only scientists exploring the use of CRISPR. Custom sheep, fish, insects, and anything else you could think of. Geneticists weren't just scientists anymore, we turned into artists, architects, building and painting with cells. Polka dot fish, phoenix-colored falcons, horses with cloven hooves.

It was only a matter of time before there was a custom human.

We went backward instead; religious fanatics all over the world got in the way. They screamed and ranted about the natural beauty of who we are, how we shouldn't be playing God, and potentially devastating consequences up to and including being smited.

I'm pretty sure the US government came up with the laws they did simply to shut up all the high-pitched screeching. That doesn't mean people don't play around with genetics. There are just a few, overly broad, limitations.

1. No humans. Ever. Never ever.
2. Plant modification can't be visible and must have a purpose. Your GMO sweet corn is safe.

3. Everything must be natural. That is, nothing that wouldn't happen through the naturally occurring process of getting down with a member of the opposite sex.

So no dogs with three heads or goldfish with shark fins. Goodbye unicorn. Goodbye Brain the Rat version two.

You can't do anything fun, essentially. You also can forget about making sure your child doesn't have Downs Syndrome. Not that I don't know people who could make that happen. Great technology, great ideas, they're all snuffed and limited.

Still, I make my living playing with genetic sequences.

You wouldn't know it, looking at me. I'm overweight by at least a hundred pounds, balding, with short and pudgy fingers. I'm the type of guy you wouldn't want to sit next to on a plane, but I'm great at what I do.

Most people looking for genetically modified animals are farmers or show breeders. Me, I'm the go-to person for show cats east of the Mississippi.

A typical first-time client will call me and make noises of understanding when I tell them what I'll need. A bit of sperm and a female cat. Or a few eggs, sperm, and the surrogate cat mom if you want to go that route. They used to all balk at my price, and sometimes first-time clients still do, but word has gotten around. I choose the genes that make high-class cats, show winners. I'm worth the high price.

But, often, I get bored. I'm a creative soul in my fat heart and that means I break a few laws.

Not on cats, mind you. That's rather obvious and would get out pretty quick. Before you know it, The Man would be pounding on my door, my business ruined, and me along with it. Government underground prisons are things I want to avoid, thank you very much. I need my sunlight and computers.

Instead, like most DNArtists as we call ourselves, I play with plants. I create plaid tulips and lilies that smell like bacon. Rose bushes with no thorns. I have a mini maple tree that doesn't lose its leaves. They all sit around my house, a credit to my talent with gene swapping and reading nucleotides. I share my codes on the DNArtists forum while others share theirs. I'd love to have the bush that produces every berry plus tangerines, but my little yard with the low fences wouldn't hide it, and I don't trust the goodwill of my neighbors enough to not report me.

But the monogrammed iris that changes color depending on the temperature like a mood ring might have been a bit much.

I was helping Helen Rodgers, Persian cat owner from Tampa, and she was such a regular client I didn't have to go through the options with her. I already knew what she wanted. Helen kept staring at the iris in the window, pink petals near the sun-warmed glass and dusky purple ones on the other side of the blossom. The giant "S" that darker chlorophyll had formed on each leaf.

"Scott, I was hoping you might be up for a different type of job today."

I only offer one type of job, because that's what I'm legally allowed to do. See, when reproducing, any creature gives half its DNA to the kid. You're 50% mom, 50% dad. What that 50% is depends on several factors - which egg or sperm make you, recessive traits versus dominate ones, and particular alleles working together. Calico coats are a good example, different patches of fur color are a result of pockets of different gene activations. And then there's the likelihood of crossover at conception when the sperm and egg meet and the little fertilized cell starts multiplying like crazy to become a recognizable embryo.

What I'm allowed to do is compare the possible children that would result from a meeting of sperms and eggs. Which little zygote will most likely win a show? Egg 1 with Sperm 5, or Egg 3 with Sperm 1? Of course, I do a bit of tweaking once I decide which couple will have the superior show-stopping child. Only naturally possible ones, of course, even if they wouldn't happen without a push from me and my code.

That's all I'm legally able to do. And I'm bored out of my mind.

Helen kept staring at the iris.

"What type of job?" I asked, staring at the petals too.

"I'd pay triple, no worries, and I promise not to tell a soul, but, see, I want to develop a new breed and would like to customize the look."

"Do you know what traits you want?" I asked

"Mostly, yes. But it might be a while collecting samples from all of the breeds," Helen replied.

"Call me when you have them."

She turned, looking away from the iris. "Is that a yes? You'll take the job?"

I shrugged, and she smiled. Legal restrictions bound me to say no, but I wanted to say yes, so I didn't say anything.

Helen got the message.

#####

It was another three months before I heard from Helen. I hadn't forgotten about her proposed job but figured she had changed her mind. I, however, had been talking to a guy on the forums about developing the DNA for a flying cat with leathery skin that could serve as a gargoyle. All hypothetical, of course. I need my intellectual puzzles.

Anyway, Helen called, and I said I was free over the weekend. She came over promptly at 3 pm on Friday with glass vials in her purse. Skin samples and blood from her own Persian.

"I want it to have Mary Weather's face. That's a breed requirement."

I always thought Persians had ugly faces, Mary Weather more than most, but oh well.

I spent the weekend staring at my computer screen, running models to show the phenotypes of the resulting cats. Helen sat on the chair next to me, accepting or nixing the fine details of tail foof and potential meow sounds based on tailored larynxes.

The approved cat had Mary Weather's scrunched face, but the less crazy hair of a Ragdoll, the coat color limited to that of a Siamese with the body of an Abyssinian. Not to mention the long ears of a Sphynx and a tail that could only belong to a Javenese. She was pleased, that's what mattered, even if I found the computer simulation of the breed outright ugly.

There was no way she would ever be able to say she bred the cat over a few generations. It was too odd a mix. That cat would never evolve naturally and it can't set a paw into a show arena. I'll never understand rich people. Doesn't stop me from taking their money though.

I told Helen it was the most beautiful cat I'd ever seen. I also told her this cat had to live in a bag and was never allowed out. She threatened to have Mary Weather eat my iris.

It took me a while to recreate a double helix matching the one we had cobbled together on the computer; conception crossovers were a nightmare. Then I stuck the fertilized eggs into Mary Weather so she could be the proud birth mom of a new breed.

It didn't work. The new breed might have had Mary Weather's face, but the body type was different and so the Persian's body attacked and destroyed the zygotes. Helen brought me an Abyssinian surrogate and this time the eggs took.

Two and a half months later, Helen sent me a photo of her new multi-crossbreed. With its matted fur and closed eyes, it wasn't exactly attractive. But hey, the kitten was healthy. Helen got what she paid for.

And I got a little bonus. Usually, a show cat will give birth to two, maybe three modified kittens instead of the five a natural genetic soup mix could result in. I expected the surrogate to have only one. But no, it was a litter of three, so now I have an illegal cat that nibbles on my illegal plants.

I named him Frankie.

#####

Frankie is a menace in two ways. One, he is rather fond of chewing my bacon-scented plants and then meowing obnoxiously when they didn't taste like delicious pork. Two, he makes me think of Brain and that makes me itch.

See, creating Frankie was easy. He's all cat-code, DNA sequencing I can identify by sight and tell you where in the chain it's found and what it interacts with. Brain had been harder, manipulating rat DNA to get specific mutations and a structured trigger of fur growth to create his patterned fur. And then we added a touch of plankton. For the bioluminescence.

I want to do more than show cats.

But I have to start small. Frankie can hide in the house, and a very good lawyer can argue that he is possible, even if rare. After all, those in the *Felis* genus are known to interbreed. Recreating Brian would have problems, I wasn't sure I could without access to the tech I did as a student, but what if I moved up the taxonomy chart? Merge *Felis* with say, a closely related family. *Pantherinae* would do. And if that worked, it'd take a few tries based on how Helen's new breed needed the right mother, why not move up to a suborder mix of those under *Feliformia?*

I sent a message to the DNArtist I'd been talking to about gargoyles. I sent a separate text to Helen.

Do you want Mary Weather to be the face of a brand-new panther?

Publication Notes

The majority of these stories have been published before, be it in other anthologies or shared online via my blogs or social media channels. Others, like *DNArtist* are completely new and this is the first time the public gets a chance to read them.

Some of these stories are related – *Not Myself Tonight* – was originally written for a blogging even back in 2013, but the idea stuck with me and transformed into *Self-Defense* which was later published in 2021.

This anthology wouldn't be possible if not for all the editors who saw something in my stories and decided to buy them, the people of Tumblr sharing my stories they liked, and the fellow writers, friends, and family who have encouraged my writing.

If you enjoyed this collection yourself, please leave a review and call out your favorite story!

Thank you all!

-

Previous Market Publications:
Confessions, The Love Anthology, 2019
Multilinear Memories, Today, Tomorrow, Always, 2019
Protecting the House, Stranded, 2020
Self-Defense, Masks, Facades, and Reveals, 2021

About the Author

Gwen Tolios is a Chicago-based author, staring at excel sheets by day and writing at night while trying to coax her cat to cuddle. While she got her start in short stories, Gwen has also written novels for children and adults.

For more short stories, please follow Gwen on Tumblr where she publishes short stories every month. For social media links and more, visit https://linktr.ee/gwentolios

www.ingramcontent.com/pod-product-compliance
Lightning Source LLC
Chambersburg PA
CBHW061223210726
48294CB00006B/1956